THE SAND ELEPHANT

Rinna Hermann and Sanne Dufft

Floris
Books

There was no one to play with.

Paul sighed, put aside his bucket and spade, and drew in the sand with his hands and feet. Soon something big was taking shape. But what was it?

Four large legs, one enormous ear, a long trunk … An elephant!

"I wish you were real and we could play together," sighed Paul, patting the elephant's great sandy head.

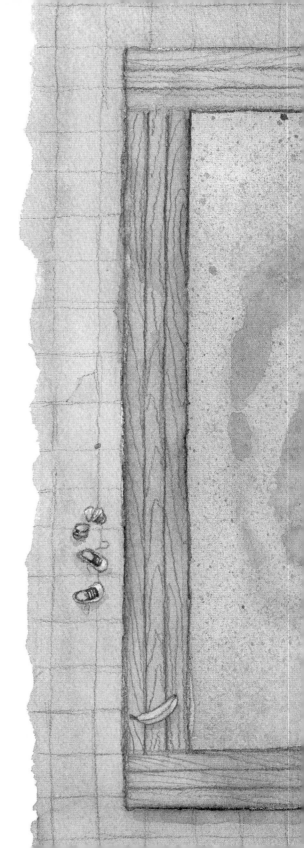

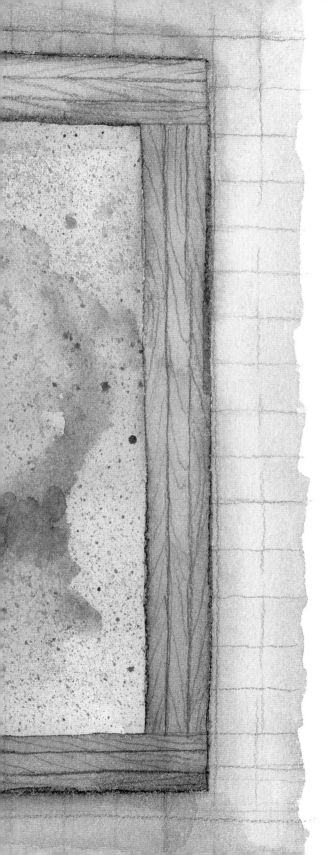

He nestled snugly under the soft curve of the elephant's trunk. It was cosy there. He was feeling drifty and dreamy when he heard a quiet snuffling sound.

"That's enough dozing," said a deep voice. "Come on, Paul! Shall I carry you on my back?" Then the elephant pushed back in a gigantic stretch that sent sand in all directions. It wrapped its trunk around Paul and lifted him up!

Perched comfortably behind the sand elephant's head, Paul could feel its back scratchy and warm like a summer beach under his bare feet.

"Let's go and play!" shouted the elephant cheerfully. "Hold tight!" Then it trumpeted:

Shell dust, coral dust, stardust, SAND!
Sand form, sandstorm, Sandcastle Land!

And it stamped its big feet, kicking up a tremendous sand cloud.

Paul closed his eyes.

Then suddenly, all was still.

Paul peered through his fingers…

In front of them
stood a magnificent
sandcastle. There were
children climbing all over it,
and sand animals meowed,
honked and snorted from every wall
and archway.

Children ran up to pat the elephant and
welcome Paul. He clambered and slid and played
with them in the sand. The air was full of laughter.

Paul laughed along with the others. He scrambled higher and higher until he found himself at the top of a ladder leaning on the tallest tower. He called to everyone below. "I'm the king of the castle!"

But the sand cockerel on the tower roof crowed:

Cock-a-doodle-doodle-doo!
I'm even higher up than you!

"I'm sure I can get there too!" Paul replied. He stepped to the top rung of the ladder, balanced, and was about to climb up next to the surprised cockerel, when …

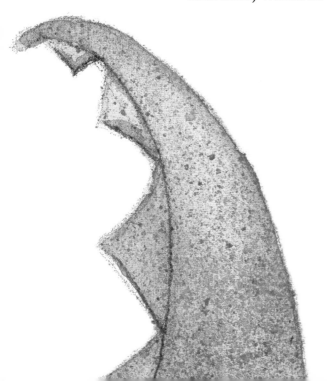

...he slipped –

whoops!

– and
tumbled –

oof!

– somersaulting down the tower
and the walls and the ramparts,
in a great cascade of sand,
whirling over and over until
he flopped –

thump!

– onto the ground.

"Don't worry, I'm okay," he mumbled, as the other children ran up. "But what about the castle? I've knocked over half the tower!"

"It's fine, Paul," rumbled the sand elephant. "Sand doesn't mind about tumbles and collapses. You should see us sand animals after it rains!"

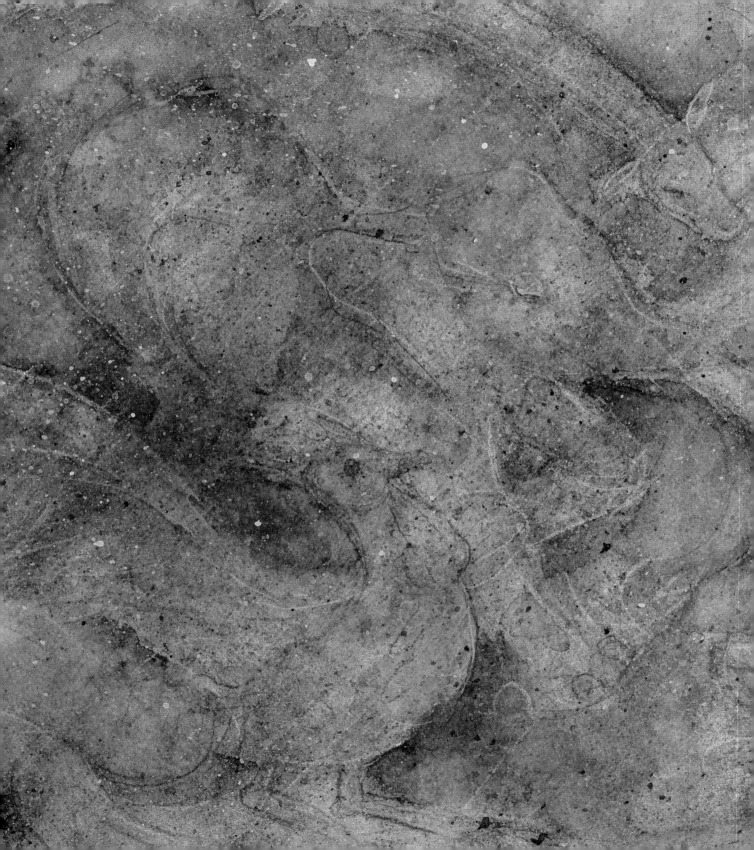

Before Paul could ask what that meant, there was a mighty gust of wind.

All the other children cheered. A storm was coming!

The sand animals leapt and danced to the thundering roar, until they mixed in a wild, swirling rush …

"Elephant!" shouted Paul. "Don't go, sand elephant!"

He heard the elephant trumpeting to him.

Then – *splash!*

Rain came.

Splish!

Splash!

Everything dripped and leaked and ran.

When the wind dropped and the rain stopped,
Paul wiped the sand from his eyes and saw a
blue summer sky, washed clean by the storm.
But around the children the sand was flat.

"It's all gone! Where's my elephant?" Paul
hurried to dig, with tears in his eyes. "I've got
to find it!"

Then a little girl said, "Let's call them!"
And the children shouted together:

Shell dust, coral dust, stardust, SAND!
Sand form, sandstorm, Sandcastle Land!

Up rose the sand animals, bounding joyfully to their friends.
   "Now do you see? Wind and rain and tumbles will never
get the better of us!" explained the sand elephant, ruffling
Paul's hair with his trunk.
   Paul smiled.

"All we sand animals need," continued the elephant, "are children who come and play in the sand again. We might look different to the last time you saw us, but you'll know us – even if we're funnier!"

It shook its head till sand sprayed everywhere, then it sprouted …

...enormous rabbit ears!

From behind the little girl, they heard:

Cock-a-doodle-doodle-doo!
Have a laugh at my shape too!

There stood the cockerel with even more
ridiculous ears.

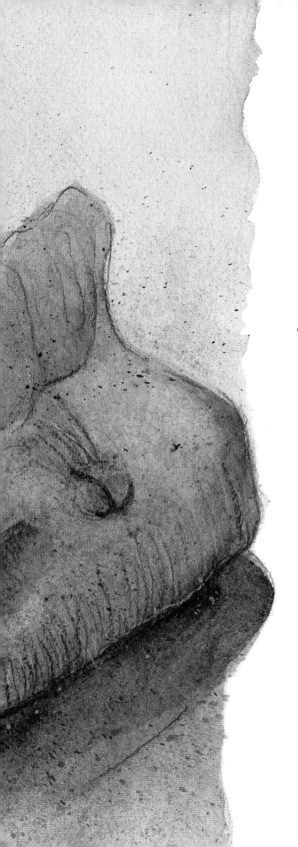

The children and the sand animals dug and built and climbed and tumbled until they were tired out.

The sand elephant lay down.

"Paul," it said, "I'm always here when you want to play."

Paul snuggled into the curve of his elephant's trunk and yawned.

The elephant rumbled softly:

Shell dust, coral dust, stardust, sand,
Come back soon to Sandcastle Land...

"Sleep tight, sand elephant," whispered Paul.

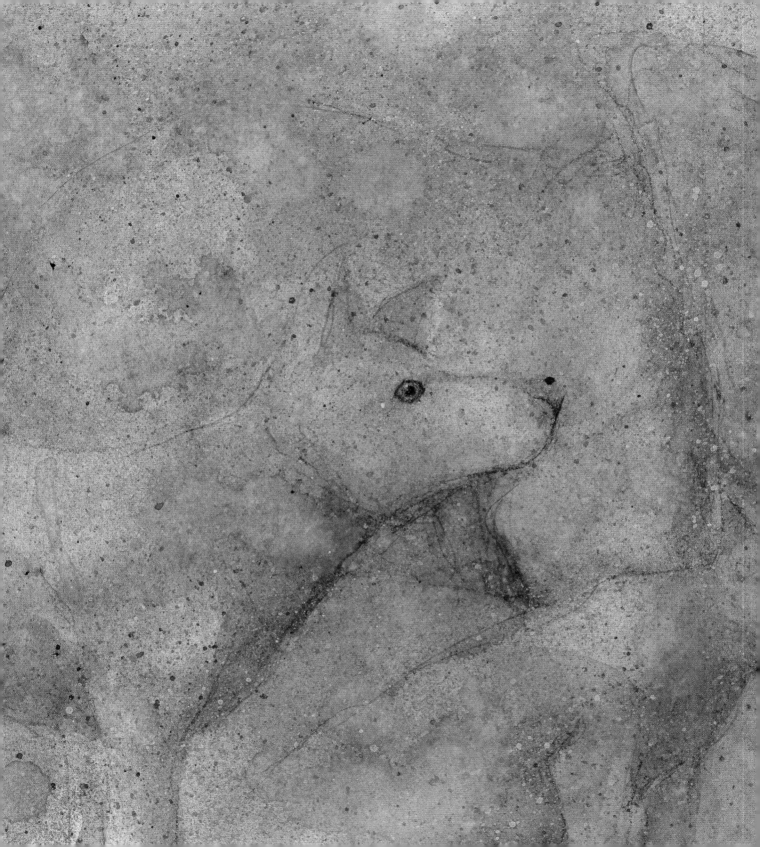

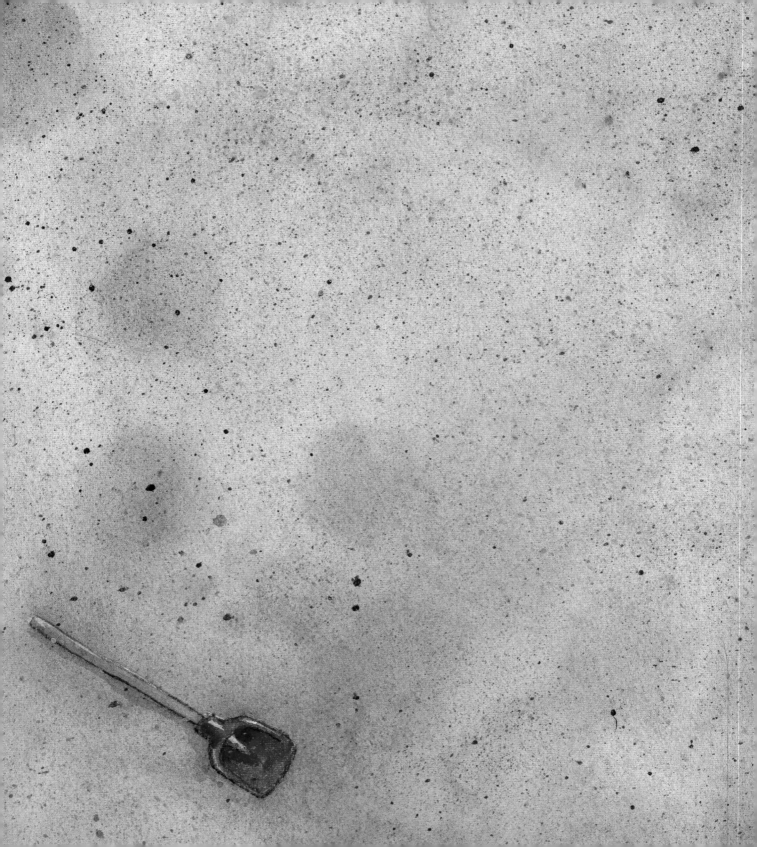